What Tiggers Do Best

Adapted from a story by Hallie Marshall

Illustrations by John Kurtz

One morning, Kanga wanted to get things done around the house. So the first thing she did was send Tigger and Roo outdoors to play in the sunshine.

Tigger bounced along, going *BOING! BOING! BOING!* And Roo followed as well as he could: *boing, boing, boing, boing!*

All that time, Tigger was talking about—tiggers. Tiggers could ice-skate and tiggers could swim, and they could even climb trees. Because a tigger, he said, could *bounce* from one branch to the next.

When the friends had gone to the top of a tree, Tigger remembered something. As good as tiggers are at bouncing upward, they don't like to climb down.

Tigger and Roo were stuck!

It was Christopher Robin who came up with a rescue plan. He took off his coat, and he and Kanga and Piglet and Pooh and Rabbit all held tight to the corners.

Roo jumped from a branch and fell safely into the middle of the coat.

"Whee!" he squealed. "Come on, Tigger. It's easy!"

Tigger looked down. "Jumping might be easy for jumping animals like kangas and roos, but it's different for bouncing animals like tiggers."

He held on to the tree for dear life.

Then Tigger slipped, and he found out how easy going down was. Once he was safe on the ground, Tigger felt like bouncing with joy, and bouncing, and bouncing, and bouncing!

Rabbit watched as Tigger bounced and bounced and bounced.

"But that's all wrong!" Rabbit said, throwing his hands in the air. "One can't go bouncing everywhere! Someone might get hurt!"

Piglet nearly agreed. Tigger had a way of saying hello that almost always bowled him over.

"We have to do something!" Rabbit said.

"But what?" Pooh asked.

"I'll circulate a petition," Rabbit announced. "Something to the effect that bouncing is bad—very, very, very bad.

"Everyone will sign it," Rabbit continued. "And the petition will be a rule: NO BOUNCING!" He smiled at the thought. "Tigger will have to stop bouncing."

Meanwhile, Pooh's eyes were partly closed. He was thinking of a hum, and was just deciding that "pounces" might sound nice with "bounces."

Tigger sometimes
Pounces Rabbit
Or bounces me
Or Piglet or Roo,
And occasionally Eeyore, too.
(And . . . bother!
This isn't going anywhere!)

"Were you humming something helpful, Pooh?" Rabbit asked.

"No, no, not at all," Pooh said. "What were you saying, Rabbit?"

Pooh hadn't been listening, but Piglet had. "Bouncing is not *that* bad," Piglet said. Then Piglet did a very brave thing indeed. He shook his head. "I won't."

Rabbit was surprised. "Won't what, little Piglet?" he asked.

"I won't sign a p-p-p-rule about bouncing. Tigger just *is* bouncy," Piglet explained. "He can't help it."

"Hmph!" said Rabbit, deciding not to make a petition after all.

"That's right, Ol' Long Ears," Tigger said. "Besides, bouncing *is* what tiggers do best! Hoo-hoo-hoo!"